' "What about me?" said that extremely small voice. "You haven't asked me what *I'm* going to be when I grow up."

The Labrador yawned.

"Oh, all right," it said. "Tell us if you must."

"I," said the sixth puppy proudly, "am going to be a guard-dog."

At this the others began to roll helplessly about, yapping and yelping and snorting with glee.

"A guard-dog!" they cried.

"Mind your ankles, burglars!"

"He's not tall enough to reach their ankles!" '

Although the guard-dog is small and very cute, his bark is anything but! Will anyone want to buy him from the pet shop? Could anyone put up with such a racket? To the surprise of the other puppies, the guard-dog is the first to be sold . . .

YOUNG CORGI BOOKS

Young Corgi books are perfect when you are looking for great books to read on your own. They are full of exciting stories and entertaining pictures and can be tackled with confidence. There are funny books, scary books, spine-tingling stories and mysterious ones. Whatever your interests you'll find something in Young Corgi to suit you: from ponies to football, from families to ghosts. The books are written by some of the most famous and popular of today's children's authors, and by some of the best new talents, too.

Whether you read one chapter a night, or devour the whole book in one sitting, you'll love Young Corgi books. The more you read, the more you'll want to read! Why not try:

All Because of Jackson
Connie and Rollo
E.S.P.
The Guard Dog
Horse Pie
Omnibombulator
The Dick King-Smith Collection
(includes E.S.P., The Guard Dog and Horse Pie)

Published by Corgi Pups
Happy Mouseday

Published by Doubleday/Corgi Yearling
A Mouse Called Wolf
Harriet's Hare
Mr Ape
Billy the Bird

Published by Corgi
The Crowstarver
Godhanger

Published by Corgi (Poetry)
Dirty Gertie Mackintosh illustrated by Ros Asquith

THE
GUARD
DOG

DICK KING-SMITH

Illustrated by Jocelyn Wild

YOUNG CORGI

THE GUARD DOG
A YOUNG CORGI BOOK : 0 552 52731 9

First published in Great Britain by Doubleday Books,
a division of Transworld Publishers

PRINTING HISTORY
Doubleday edition published 1991
Young Corgi edition published 1992

20

Young Corgi Books are published by Transworld Publishers,
61–63 Uxbridge Road, London W5 5SA,
a division of The Random House Group Ltd,
in Australia by Random House Australia (Pty) Ltd,
20 Alfred Street, Milsons Point, Sydney, NSW 2061, Australia,
in New Zealand by Random House New Zealand Ltd,
18 Poland Road, Glenfield, Auckland 10, New Zealand
and in South Africa by Random House (Pty) Ltd,
Endulini, 5a Jubilee Road, Parktown 2193, South Africa.

Printed and bound in Great Britain by
Cox & Wyman Ltd, Reading, Berkshire

CONTENTS

Chapter One   9

Chapter Two   21

Chapter Three   29

Chapter Four   47

THE GUARD DOG

Chapter 1

There were six puppies in the window of the pet shop. People who know about dogs would have easily recognized their breeds. There was a Labrador, a springer spaniel, an Old

9

English sheepdog, a poodle and a pug.

But even the most expert dog-fancier couldn't have put a name to the sixth one. In fact, most of those who stopped to look in the pet shop window either didn't notice it (because it was so extremely small) or thought it was a rough-haired guinea-pig (which it resembled in size and shape) that had got into the wrong pen.

'What on earth is that?' the rest had said to one another when the sixth puppy was first put in with them. 'Looks like something the cat dragged in!' And they sniggered amongst themselves.

'I say!' said the Old English sheep-dog puppy loudly. 'What *are* you?'

The newcomer wagged a tail the length of a pencil-stub.

'I'm a dog,' it said in an extremely small voice.

The pug snorted.

'You could have fooled me,' said the poodle.

'Do you mean,' said the Labrador, 'that you're a dog, as opposed to a bitch?'

'Well, yes.'

'But what sort of dog?' asked the springer spaniel.

'How d'you mean, what sort?'

The pug snorted again, and then they all started barking questions.

'What breed are you?'

'What variety of dog?'

'Why are you so small?'

'Why are you so hairy?'

'Are you registered with the Kennel Club?'

'How many champions have you in your pedigree?'

'Pedigree?' said the sixth puppy. 'What's a pedigree?'

There was a stunned silence, broken at last by a positive volley of snorts.

'Pshaw!' said the pug. 'He's a mongrel!'

At that they all turned their backs and began to talk among themselves.

'I say!' said the Labrador. 'D'you know what I'm going to be when I grow up?'

13

'A gun-dog, I bet,' said the springer spaniel, 'like me. I'm going to be a gun-dog and go out with my master and bring back the pheasants he shoots.'

'No,' said the Labrador, 'as a matter of fact I'm not. I'm going to be a guide-dog for the blind. A much more worthwhile job.'

'No more worthwhile than mine,' said the Old English sheepdog. 'I'm going to work sheep. I'll be galloping about all over the countryside . . .'

'. . . getting filthy dirty,' interrupted the poodle, 'while I'm having my coat shampooed and specially trimmed and clipped, and a silk ribbon tied in my topknot. I'm going to be a show-dog and win masses of prizes.'

The pug snorted.

'What about you?' barked the others. 'You haven't said what you're going to be when you grow up.'

'I am going to be a lap-dog,' said the pug loftily. 'I shall be thoroughly spoiled and eat nothing but chicken and steak, and the only exercise I shall take will be to walk to my food-dish. Pshaw!'

'What about me?' said that extremely small voice. 'You haven't asked me what *I'm* going to be when I grow up.'

The Labrador yawned.

'Oh, all right,' it said. 'Tell us if you must.'

'I,' said the sixth puppy proudly, 'am going to be a guard-dog.'

At this the others began to roll helplessly about, yapping and yelping and snorting with glee.

'A guard-dog!' they cried.

'Mind your ankles, burglars!'

'He's not tall enough to reach their ankles!'

'If he did, those little teeth would only tickle them!'

'Perhaps his bark is worse than his bite!'

'It is!' said the sixth puppy. 'Listen!'

Then, out of his hairy little mouth came the most awful noise you can possibly imagine. It was a loud noise, a very very loud noise for such a tiny animal, but its volume was nothing like as awful as its tone.

Think of these sounds: chalk scraping on a blackboard, a wet finger squeaking on a window-pane, a hacksaw cutting through metal, rusty door-hinges creaking, an angry baby screaming, and throw in the horribly bubbly sound of someone with a really nasty cough. Mix them all up together and there you have the noise that the sixth puppy made.

It was a dreadful noise, a revolting

disgusting jarring vulgar noise, and it set all the creatures in the pet shop fluttering and scuttering about in panic. As for the other puppies, they bunched together as far away as they could get, their hackles raised, their lips wrinkled in loathing.

At last, after what seemed an age, the sixth puppy stopped. Head on one side, he wagged his pencil-stub tail.

'You see,' he said happily in his usual extremely small voice. 'I can make quite a rumpus when I really try.'

Chapter 2

'Nobody will buy him,' said the other puppies later. 'That's for sure.'

'What a racket!' said the sheepdog.

'It made me feel quite ill!' said the gun-dog.

'A really common noise!' said the guide-dog.

'Made by a really common animal!' said the show-dog.

'Pshaw!' said the lap-dog.

They all stared balefully at the guard-dog.

'The sooner he's sold, the better,' they said.

And that afternoon, he was.

Into the pet shop walked a tall lady with a face that looked as though it had a bad smell under its nose, and a small fat girl.

'I am looking for a puppy,' said the lady to the shopkeeper, 'for my daughter. I know nothing about dogs. Which of these would you recommend?'

All the puppies lolloped forward to the inner wire of the pen, whining and wagging and generally looking as irresistible as puppies do. All, that is, except the guard-dog. He sat alone, small and silent. He was not exactly

sulking — that was not in his nature —
but he still felt very hurt.

'Nobody will buy him. That's for
sure,' they had said.

He resigned himself to life in a pet
shop.

The shopkeeper was busy explain-
ing the various virtues of the five
pedigree puppies when the fat child,
who was standing, sucking her
thumb, took it out with a plop.

She pointed at the guard-dog.

'Want that one,' she said.

'Oh, that's just a mongrel puppy,
dear,' said the shopkeeper. 'I expect
Mummy would prefer . . .'

'Want that one.'

'But, darling . . .'

The small fat girl stamped her small fat foot. She frowned horribly. She hunched her shoulders. With a movement that was as sudden as it was decisive, she jammed her thumb back in her small fat mouth.

'She wants that one,' said her mother.

By the end of that day, the guard-dog was feeling pretty pleased with life.

To be sure, there were things about his new owners that he did not quite understand. It seemed, for example, that simple pleasures like chewing carpets and the bottom edges of curtains drove the lady into what he considered a quite unreasonable rage, and as for the child, she was temperamental, he thought, to say the least.

Though at first she had seemed

willing to play with him, she soon began to complain that his teeth were too sharp or his claws too scratchy or his tongue too slobbery, and had made a ridiculous fuss over a doll which had sported a fine head of hair and was now bald.

Strange creatures, he thought that night when at last all was quiet, but I mustn't grumble. I'm warm and well-fed and this seems a very fine house for a guard-dog to guard. Which reminds me — it's time I was off on my rounds.

Ears cocked, nose a-quiver, he pattered off on a tour of the downstairs rooms.

His patrol over, he settled down in a basket in the kitchen. There was plain evidence that he had done his duty. In the centre of the drawing-room, for example, there was a fine white fleecy rug, and in the centre of the rug was a bright yellow pool. In other rooms there were other messes.

Comfortable now, the guard-dog closed his extremely small eyes. It had been a tiring day, and he was just drifting off to sleep when suddenly, outside the kitchen door, he heard a stealthy sound! He leaped to his feet.

Chapter 3

Afterwards the family could not understand why their cat would never again enter the house, but lived, timidly, in the garden shed. They did not know that its nerves had been shattered by the simple act of pressing against the cat-flap, something it had done every day of its life. This had resulted instantly in a noise that sounded to its horrified ears like a number of cats being scrunched up in a giant mincer. Upstairs, the fat child woke screaming, and soon her mother came rushing down those stairs and stepped in something un-usual at the bottom.

Even then the guard-dog might still have had a house to guard (for it was difficult for them to believe that so little a creature was capable of making so ghastly a noise), if only he had kept his mouth shut the next morning.

But he stuck to his task, challeng-ing everything that seemed to him a threat to the territory which it was his duty to protect. Quite early, at the sound of whistling and the chink of

bottles outside the door, he woke his owners once more. And no sooner had they taken the milk in than the postman knocked, and they actually saw the guard-dog in action.

Happily unaware of the effect of his voice upon the human ear, and mindful only of his role — to give warning of the approach of strangers — the guard-dog kept it up all morning.

The cleaning woman (who found a great deal of cleaning to do), the paper boy, the electricity man come to read the meter, and a door-to-door salesman were each in turn greeted by the dreadful medley of sounds that emerged, full blast, from the guard-dog's tiny throat. Last came a collector for the RSPCA, the rattle of whose tin inspired the guard-dog to his loudest, longest and most furious outburst.

'RSPCA?' screamed his distracted owner. 'What about a society for the

prevention of
cruelty to people?'
And at midday,
as she unscrewed
the Aspirin bottle,
she said to her
daughter, 'I'm
sorry, darling,
but I cannot
stand that row
a moment longer.
It'll have to go.
Will you be very
upset?'

The small fat girl, her eyes fixed
malevolently upon the guard-dog,
did not even bother to remove her
thumb from her mouth. She merely
shook her head, violently.

That afternoon the guard-dog found himself, to his surprise, in a very different kind of home — the Dogs' Home. He could not make out what had gone wrong. What were guard-dogs meant to do if not guard? He had only done his duty, but all he had received so far had been angry looks and angry words before finally they bundled him into their car, and drove him to a strange place full of strange dogs and left him.

From the kennel he had been given, Number 25, he looked round him. There was every sort of dog in the kennel block, young and old, handsome and ugly, large and small (though none remotely as small as he). Why were they all there?

'Why are we all here?' he asked the dog directly opposite him, a sad-looking animal with long droopy ears and a long droopy face.

'Because,' said the dog dolefully, 'we are all failures.'

I don't get it, thought the guard-dog. My job is to give warning of the approach of strangers. I've never yet failed in that.

'I don't think I'm a failure,' he said.

'Well, you're certainly not a success,' said the long-faced dog, 'or you wouldn't be here. All of us are here because our owners couldn't stand us any longer.'

'But we'll get new owners, won't we?'

'Possibly. It depends.'

'Depends on what?'

'On whether you take someone's fancy. You just have to do whatever you're best at. Me, I'm best at looking sad. Some people like that.'

In the days that followed, many people in search of a suitable pet came

to inspect the twenty or so current inmates of the Dogs' Home; and when they came to the end of the range of kennels and found the smallest inhabitant, they would without exception break into smiles at the

sight of such a charming little scrap.

Without exception, however, they were treated to the dreadful spectacle of the guard-dog doing what he was best at. And without exception the smiles vanished, to be replaced by

looks of horror as they turned away
with their hands clapped to their ears.

By the time the guard-dog had
been in the Dogs' Home for a week,
most of the animals had gone happily

(or in the case of the long-faced dog, sadly) away with new owners, and there were newcomers in most of the kennels.

By the thirteenth day, there was only one dog left of those who had been there when he was admitted. This was his next-door neighbour, an old and rather smelly terrier.

The guard-dog's attempts to make conversation with it had always thus far been met with a surly growl, so he was quite surprised when he was suddenly addressed.

'You bin in 'ere thirteen days, littl'un, an't you?' said the terrier.

'Oh,' said the guard-dog, 'have I?'

'Ar. You come in day after I. 'Tis my fourteenth day.'

'Oh well,' said the guard-dog, 'try not to worry. I'm sure you'll soon be gone.'

'Ar,' said the terrier. 'I shall. To-day.'

'But how can you know that? How can you know that someone's going to take you away today?'

'Fourteen days is the limit, littl'un. They don't keep you no longer than that.'

'Why, what do they do with you then?'

'An't nobody told you?'

'No.'

'Ar well,' said the old terrier. ''Tis all right for us old uns, 'tis time to go. I shan't be sorry. You don't feel nothing, they do say. But 'tis a shame for a nipper like you.'

'I don't understand,' said the guard-dog. 'What are you trying to tell me?' But though he kept on asking, the old dog only growled at him, and then lay silent, staring blankly out of its kennel. Later, a man in a white coat came and led it gently away.

Chapter 4

'Oh, thanks,' said the manager of
the Dogs' Home, when one of his
kennelmaids brought in his cup of
coffee at eleven o'clock next morning. He looked up from his record
book.

'Shame about that little titchy one in Number twenty-five,' he said.

'You don't mean . . .?' said the kennelmaid.

''Fraid so. If things had been slack we could have kept him longer, but the way dogs are pouring in, we must keep to the two-week rule. He's one for the vet today.'

'Oh dear,' said the kennelmaid. 'He's such a lovely little fellow. Dozens of people fell for him, until . . .'

' . . . until he opened his mouth,' said the manager. 'I know. It's a pity, but you can't blame them. In all my long experience of every sort of dog, I've never come across one with such a dreadful voice. Nobody could possibly live with that; though, talk about burglar alarms — any burglar would run a mile if he heard that hullabaloo. And you wouldn't need to dial nine-nine-nine — they'd hear it at the nearest police station easy.'

The guard-dog ate a hearty breakfast, and was a little surprised when the kennelmaid came to clean out his run,

at the fuss she made of him. She cuddled and stroked and kissed him as if she would never see him again.

Then he remembered what the smelly old terrier had said. This is my fourteenth day, he thought. Great! Someone will pick me out today! He sat, waiting for the time when the public were admitted, determined that today of all days he would leave no-one in any doubt as to the quality of his greatest asset. Other guard-dogs, he supposed, might act in other ways, by looking large and fierce (which he could not) or by leaping up and planting their feet on the shoulders of burglars and suchlike and knocking them flat (which he

most certainly could not). He had only his voice, and when the door to the kennel block opened, he let rip, fortissimo.

No-one even got to smiling at him that morning. Everybody kept as far away as possible from the dreadful sounds issuing from Number 25, and concentrated upon the other inmates. The guard-dog was left strictly alone.

When at last the batch of would-be owners had left, some with new companions, some empty-handed, all mightily relieved to reach the comparative peace and quiet of the busy roaring street outside, the guard-dog sat silent once more. There was a puzzled look on his extremely small and hairy face.

Can't understand it, he thought. Nobody seems to want a decent guard-dog. But if fourteen days was the limit, then they'd jolly well have to find him somewhere to go today. Perhaps the man in the white coat would take him too — he'd seemed a nice sort of chap.

He watched the door to the kennel block.

It was not the man in the white coat who came in but the kennelmaid with a man with white hair, who walked with a stick with a rubber tip to it.

'Would you like me to come round with you?' the kennelmaid said, but

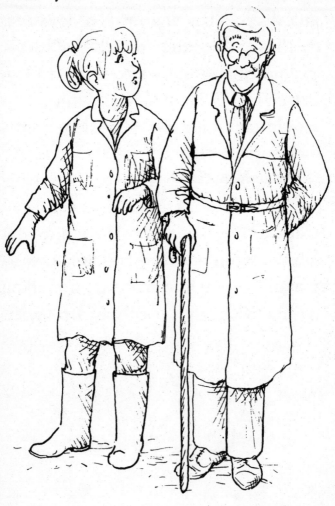

he did not answer, so she went away and left him alone.

The old man walked slowly along the row of kennels, looking carefully into each with sharp blue eyes. At last he came to Number 25.

Outside the door, the kennelmaid stood listening, her fingers tightly crossed. But then she heard that fearful noise start up and shook her head sadly.

She went back into the kennel block to find the old man squatting on his heels. There was a grin on his face as he looked, apparently totally unmoved, at the howling bawling yowling squalling guard-dog. He levered himself to his feet.

'I'll have this little fellow,' he said firmly. 'He's the boy for me.'

'Oh good!' cried the kennelmaid. 'He's lovely, don't you think?' But the old man did not answer.

He did not reply later either, when he had paid for the guard-dog and the kennelmaid said, 'Would you like a box to carry him in?' And in answer to the manager's question, 'What are

you going to call him?' he only said,
'Good afternoon.'

Light suddenly dawned on the manager of the Dogs' Home. He stood directly in front of the guard-dog's new owner so as to be sure of catching his eye, and said deliberately, in a normal tone, 'That's some dog you've got there. The worst voice in the world!'

The old man put his hand up to his ear.

'Sorry?' he said. 'Didn't catch that. I'm as deaf as a post and I can't be bothered with those hearing-aid things — never been able to get on with them. What did you say?'

'That's some dog you've got there. The best choice in the world!' said the manager very loudly.

The white-haired old man only

smiled, leaning on his stick with one
hand and cradling his purchase in the
other.

The manager shouted as loudly as he could, 'He's a dear little chappie!'

'See that he's really happy?' said the old man. 'Of course I will, you needn't worry about that. We'll be as happy as two peas in a pod.'

He fondled the puppy's extremely small hairy ears.

'Funny,' he said. 'I fell for him though he wasn't actually what I was looking for. I live all on my own, you see, so really it would have been more sensible to get a guard-dog.'

THE END

ALL BECAUSE OF JACKSON
by Dick King-Smith

'I want to sail the seas,'
said Jackson.
'I want to see the world.'

Jackson is a very unusual rabbit – a rabbit with
a dream.

He spends his days watching the tall sailing-ships
coming and going. He longs to go to sea, too. So
one day – with his girlfriend, Bunny – Jackson
stows away on the Atalanta and sails off in search
of a new life.

A fascinating and funny tale from master
storyteller Dick King-Smith, creator of *BABE*.
SMARTIES PRIZE BRONZE MEDAL WINNER

*'Dick King-Smith at his best . . . it stands reading and
re-reading, and each time you chuckle at something
different'*
THE INDEPENDENT

Published by Young Corgi Books, available from
all good bookstores.

0 552 52821 8

HORSE PIE
by Dick King-Smith

Three magnificent horses – in terrible danger . . .

Captain, Ladybird and Herbert – two Shire
horses and a Suffolk Punch – are not pleased
when Jenny, a retired seaside donkey, arrives at
the Old Horses' Home. It's supposed to be a
home for horses, and they don't want to share
their field with a common little donkey.

Then rustlers are spotted in the area: thieves who
like nothing better than to steal horses and ship
them abroad – to be made into horse pie! Can
Jenny and her friends save the huge heavy horses

A exciting adventure from master storyteller
Dick-King Smith, creator of *BABE*

Published by Young Corgi Books, available from
all good book stores.

0 552 52785 8

E.S.P.
by Dick King-Smith

'That bird,' said Old Smelly, 'picked a winner. Or should I say he pecked a winner. By making a hole. You don't suppose, do you, that that bird could have . . . known?'

Old Smelly, the tramp can hardly believe his luck when he meets young Eric Stanley Pigeon in the park. For the pigeon appears to have a very unusual talent – he can peck out the name of the winning horse from a list of runners in the newspaper. How does he do it? Could he Possibly have . . . Extra Sensory Perception? E.S.P.?

Published by Young Corgi Books, available from all good book stores.

0 552 54606 2